Truth: Flying Fox

Truth:

Flying Fox

Book B1 in the "Ethics Morals Laws" series

By Zak Maymin, Ph.D.

Truth: Flying Fox

Book B1 in the "Ethics Morals Laws" series

© 2017 Zak Maymin

truthmaymin@gmail.com

ISBN-13: 978-1974435722

ISBN-10: 1974435725

To my parents, Maria and Grigori Maymin, with love.

I am grateful to Senia, Philip, Allan, Dan, Stella, Maya, Noa, Ron, Tobin, and Zina for great comments and support.

Table of Contents

This is tea, officer

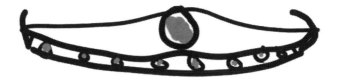

Tiara

You've decided to do something. Something not that important. You mentioned it to parents, friends, or maybe even strangers. And suddenly you hear *no*. Don't do it.

Should you listen to them? Or should you just ignore them? Of course, you should listen if they give a solid reason. Right? But what if their reasons are vague, or they don't give any reason at all? Should you follow their advice or not?

Q. Should you still do what you decided to do?

Yes. Because for any action you are going to take, you can always find somebody who tells you not to do it. And if the choice is between doing and not doing something, you may not do it just because you are lazy. Do it and don't think twice about it. Don't let other people control your life.

No. Why should you do it if it isn't that important anyway? Other people may warn you because they know something you don't, but they may not be able—for various reasons—to substantiate their warnings. What if they don't want or are not allowed to disclose their sources? What if they are not smart enough to formulate their arguments convincingly? What if they feel they did enough for you already by disclosing their concerns? Or what if their concern came from their subconscious mind, and they could not explain it rationally? If they are sincere, and you are sure that they don't have ulterior motives, why not take this into account? It is not that important for you anyway, but they apparently think the consequences might be disastrous— otherwise they presumably wouldn't have warned you.

Chloe was struggling with exactly this problem. The day before, Emma had invited Chloe to her birthday party and in just a few hours Chloe was warned not to go. By *three* different people.

First, it was her mom. After finishing her homework, Chloe ran down the stairs. She stepped into the kitchen to take her dog for a walk. She saw her mom paying bills at the table. That's when Chloe told her that she was invited to the party.

"You are a big girl, and of course it's up to you, but I wouldn't go if I were you."

"Why?"

"Because Emma is a liar and a manipulator."

"When did she lie? When did she manipulate me?" she asked, incredulous. At her feet, her little dog started whining to be taken out.

"Remember when she told you not to tell anyone that she fell? You didn't, and you lost a game because of that."

Chloe said that situation wasn't clear because it was Chloe's fault, at least initially—she had bumped into Emma and made her fall. She asked her mom to give her more examples, and her mom brought up some minor episodes from the past where Emma wasn't entirely truthful or sincere.

While Chloe was walking her dog, she called Jay, her neighbor, who was in the same class as her and Emma, and asked him whether he was going to the party. He said he wasn't invited. After a small pause, he said she shouldn't go either.

"Why shouldn't I go?" she asked.

He just repeated, "Don't go."

"Why?"

He hung up without explaining.

Chloe's dog yanked his leash as she was putting the phone away. She spun around, lost her balance, and bumped into a woman running on the sidewalk, who fell to the ground. And that's when Chloe got the weirdest warning of all.

It was a woman in her fifties, wearing black leggings, a blue jacket, and a reflective yellow vest. Chloe tightened her dog's leash and bent down to help her, but the woman, annoyed, jerked her head and turned away. She picked her white wool hat up from the ground, gave it a shake to clean it off, and put it in her back pocket. While she was doing that Chloe noticed a beautiful silver tiara on her head. The base was mounted with glittering, expensive-looking blue stones.

The woman got up and was about to resume her jog when her tiara flashed briefly with a red light. She turned and stared wordlessly at Chloe.

Chloe felt spooked and started to go when the woman said, "Don't do it." Chloe thought she was talking about the fall and said, "I'm sorry." But the woman said, "Don't go." That sounded strange, but then Chloe figured out that the woman must have heard her on the phone.

"Why not?" she asked.

"Because you are going to kill me."

18

The woman gave her a piercing look and ran off while Chloe just stood there, in shock. Strangely, the woman hadn't said, "You almost killed me," or "You will kill me you if you keep doing this." She said, "You are going to kill me." Her English was perfect, so it wasn't just a grammatical slip. And her look wasn't hatred or love; it would be best described as intense interest.

Unknown drink

"Finally, you're here!" Emma met Chloe at the door. "I have a surprise for you!"

"Surprise? Good or bad?" Chloe asked.

"Great news!" Emma pulled her inside and shut the door. Chloe was greeted by the deafening sounds of music, loud chatter, and laughter. She handed Emma a small package with a birthday gift. Inside, there was a card drawn by Chloe and a few flower pins that Chloe had picked out with great care at different stores in the mall because she knew Emma liked them.

Emma thanked her and jauntily threw the small package on a table in the hall. Chloe was glad she hadn't unwrapped it. She couldn't take her eyes off a big rose, made of precious, deep blood-red stones with a slightly bluish hue, pinned on Emma's dress.

"Are we best friends?" whispered Emma.

"What?" The music was terribly loud, but Chloe heard her, and just wasn't sure what to say.

"You are my best friend. Am I your best friend?" asked Emma louder. She was smiling, eyes wide open.

Q. Should Chloe say Emma is her best friend even though she wasn't sure it was true?

No. This is a lie. There is nothing wrong in saying something like: "We are friends, but I am not sure we are best friends."

Yes. This is a white lie. She doesn't have to start Emma's birthday party off by slighting her.

"Yes, we are best friends," said Chloe.

"Listen carefully. If you do this," Emma made two fists and, in the same motion, shot two index fingers at Chloe, "I swear to do everything you ask."

"Thank you," said Chloe, not sure whether it was the appropriate answer. "What's the big surprise?"

"Swear that you will do everything I ask, if I do this." Emma repeated the gesture. "And I'll tell you the great surprise. The biggest surprise of your life." She was bursting with excitement.

Q. Should Chloe swear?

Yes. Why turn down such an innocent request by the birthday girl? Seriously, what's Emma going to ask Chloe to do? To kill somebody with her index fingers?

No. It's a lie. Chloe should refuse to swear. Even if Emma feels offended—so be it.

"Ok," said Chloe.

"Swear!"

"I swear." Chloe smiled. Emma's excitement was contagious.

"I showed my cousin Kevin your picture and he likes you!" Emma could hardly contain herself.

"That's the surprise?"

"Don't be a little girl."

"Am I a little girl?"

"No. And don't be. Come on." A little disappointed with Chloe's inadequate response, Emma took Chloe's hand and brought her inside.

Chloe didn't recognize Emma's guests except for a handful of familiar faces she sometimes saw in their school hallways. None of those she did recognize were in her class. They were high school seniors she never talked to.

All of them had casual clothes on, like Chloe did. The difference was, and Chloe saw it right away, that their casual was much more expensive than anything Chloe ever wore, and bought in stores that Chloe never visited.

Emma hurriedly introduced her to some of the guests. And then they stood in front of Kevin. He was tall and charming and had long blond hair.

"Kevin—Chloe! Chloe—Kevin!" said Emma and ran away.

Kevin laughed at the brisk introduction and Chloe laughed back. A new song started and Kevin invited her to dance with him. It was a slow dance, and they spent the whole time chatting while swaying to the languid tempo. Kevin asked Chloe how she knew Emma and she explained they went to the same school. She asked what school he attended; he smiled and said he was in college already. Then, he asked where she lived. Chloe answered and asked him the same question. He said he lived in the governor's mansion.

"Why?" she asked.

Which turned out to be a stupid question. "Because my father is the governor." Kevin smiled again.

She felt embarrassed. He noticed and changed the topic. He said that he and his friend Eben had started a new revolutionary movement. He even asked Chloe if she wanted to join.

"What movement?"

"Property is Theft." He explained it's unfair that some people have too much and others have nothing. Chloe wasn't convinced but didn't want to argue. She said, "I'll think about it."

The song ended. Kevin thanked her and tried to kiss her, but she turned her head away.

Kevin went to the kitchen and Chloe just stood there, not sure what to do. Nobody paid any attention to her. She felt out of place. Her gift was wrong, her clothes were wrong, her conversation was wrong, and why did she turn away when he wanted her to kiss? What was the big deal?

Emma waved to her from the kitchen and Chloe joined her and Kevin there.

Emma shut the door behind her and they all sat at the breakfast table that had some cheese, nuts, crackers, and a few drinks on it. Kevin stood up and brought Chloe what he called "a special drink." It looked like tea, but smelled funny, like raw mushrooms. Kevin said it would make her feel better, more relaxed. Emma noticed Chloe's hesitation and said she had tried it and liked the feeling afterwards. "Just don't tell anyone about it," she said, smiling.

"I don't know if I want to try," said Chloe.

"She is just a little girl," mocked Emma. Somebody rang at the door and Emma, rising to meet the new guest, winked to Kevin. "She is afraid of her mommy and daddy."

27

Q. Should Chloe try the drink?

Yes. While she hasn't known Kevin for long, he is not a total stranger. He wouldn't have offered her something that could hurt her. Emma had tried it and liked it. Emma is her friend and wouldn't lie to her. Chloe should try new things.

No. This drink is unknown. Kevin and Emma could be lying. Why didn't Kevin just tell her what was in the drink? Even if they are not lying, this drink could be bad for Chloe. It's true that she should try new things in life, but she deserved to know what exactly she was about to try. And it's not important for Chloe to try it. She could at least ask her parents first.

On the one hand, Chloe liked that she was asked to keep a secret. It meant her friends trusted her. On the other hand, she was wondering what made the tea a secret. And just yesterday her mom had reminded her how Emma once asked her to keep a secret and it didn't turn out well for Chloe.

Q. Is keeping a secret a lie?

No. You made a promise and you are supposed to keep it. It's not a lie. In fact, if you gave your word and then break it, that means you lied.

Yes. That's why you should very rarely, if ever, agree to keep a secret. When you promise to keep a secret, you promise one person to lie to another person by not telling them something—something that could be very important. If somebody asks you to keep a secret, it's often a signal that whatever you are being asked to do and keep secret about is wrong.

The door opened and a policewoman came in. "Who is the resident of this house?"

"I am," said Emma. "What's the problem, officer?"

"Your neighbors complained that the music is very loud. Could you maybe turn it down a little?"

"Sure," said Emma. "We'll turn it down right away."

"Thank you," said the policewoman. "Have a nice evening."

She hesitated, then she asked Emma, "Are you above the drinking age?"

"No, but we are not drinking, officer."

"What's that drink?" She stepped toward Chloe and pointed at the glass in front of her.

Chloe stood. Across her, Kevin was frozen in his seat with sheer panic in his eyes. Behind the policewoman, Emma raised her eyebrows, begging for help. Chloe stepped aside.

In desperation, Emma shook her head *no*. Remembering something, she shot her two index fingers at Chloe. Suddenly it became very quiet. Chloe could hear water drop from a loose faucet. One drop... Another drop...

"This is tea, officer," said Chloe. She picked up the glass and drank it all.

Q. Did Chloe do the right thing by lying to the policewoman and drinking the "tea"?

No. It's not her problem. She didn't have to endanger her health and risk legal problems covering somebody else's mistakes.

Yes. The bottom line is Emma is her friend and friends should help friends when they are in trouble.

As soon as the policewoman left the kitchen with Emma, Kevin, trying to regain his confidence, asked Chloe for another dance. Chloe just slowly shook her head and Kevin also left.

All of a sudden, Chloe felt nauseous. A dripping faucet turned into unbearable dins pounding in her head. She wanted to fix it, but her legs were so heavy she just couldn't get up. She closed her eyes, put her head in her arms and sat at the table for a few minutes until she felt better.

Then she called her mom, who came and took her home.

Headache

That night, Chloe had a strong headache and couldn't not sleep at all. Whenever she had managed to close her eyes briefly, she had repeated nightmares. Nightmares of flying. And not just flying, but flying with foxes. She told her parents in the morning about her headache, but she did not tell them about the mushroom-smelling drink that she had had at Emma's.

Q. Should Chloe have told her parents about the drink?

No. Her friends asked her not to tell anyone and she made a promise. She should keep her word. Besides, telling her parents about the drink would only unnecessarily upset them. They can't do anything about it now. Anyway, she is telling them about the headache. The parents didn't ask her about the drink, so it's ok not to tell them.

Yes. This is very important information for her parents. If she doesn't tell them, she is lying. Even if the parents didn't ask about it, since they didn't know what to ask, Chloe would be lying by omission. Also, by keeping it a secret, Chloe is risking her own life; it's much harder to get the right treatment without knowing what caused the illness.

Visiting a doctor

Her dad took her to a doctor before school in his huge truck. He was a truck driver and they had to drive around finding a parking lot that would take the truck. Chloe didn't like it because it wasn't fun to drive aimlessly around and to walk a few blocks in a hot day under the sun. She didn't complain, but her dad saw that she was upset and tried to distract her by telling her that the doctor was his close friend and that's why they got the appointment right away.

A few yards in front of them, a big black bird picked something up from the sidewalk and flew away.

"Did you see that?" asked Chloe. "The bird never landed."

"Yes," said her dad. "There are some birds that don't touch the ground for several months."

"Wow, really? How do they sleep?"

"They can sleep while flying. They are called swifts."

Chloe remembered her dream and asked her dad, "Are there any foxes that could fly?"

Her dad was surprised. "Why are you asking?"

"I saw them in my dreams last night. They had black wings."

Without stopping, her dad typed something into his phone. "There are more than sixty species living in Asia, Australia,

Africa, and some Pacific Islands. The biggest is probably Acerodon jubatus, the giant golden-crowned flying fox from the Philippines."

"Acerodon jubatus? Sounds like abracadabra."

"They've been on this Earth for at least 35 million years. Be careful."

"Why?"

"The legend says," he was reading from his phone while walking, "that they can connect with other worlds at night." Her dad was smiling and it was clear that he didn't believe it.

"Acerodon?" Chloe repeated, "Jubatus?"

While they were waiting in the examining room, Chloe heard a man who seemed to be crying. He kept saying, "But doctor, they lied to me. They lied to me!"

She recognized the voice, and said to her dad, "I think it's my teacher, Mr. Kimball." Her dad got up and shut the door to their room.

In a few minutes, Dr. Acosta, their family doctor, came in. He asked Chloe a silly question that adults always ask. "Are you a good girl?"

Chloe answered with a question. "What does it mean to be a good girl?"

"Everybody knows when you are a good girl and when you are not," said the doctor. "And you know it too."

He quickly checked Chloe. He asked her if she had eaten or drunk something unusual or something that tasted bad. She said no. He prescribed some medicine. He said it was very important for Chloe to take one pill every two hours and drink a glass of water after that. He said her condition was serious, but if she did what he told her, she should be ok. He insisted that Chloe take one pill right away. And he told them that there was no need to skip school.

Her dad said, "Thank you for seeing us right away."

The doctor said, "As long as I am practicing, I'll always see you right away." He turned to Chloe. "Do you know what your father did for me?"

"No."

"He didn't tell you that?"

"No."

Chloe and her dad were sitting. But, for the first time during the appointment, the doctor sat down in a chair too. The nurse opened the door, but the doctor gestured to her that he was coming and she left. "I was driving my pregnant wife to the hospital when my car broke down. She was about to deliver a baby. I was signaling passing cars, begging for help, but nobody stopped. Suddenly a bus full of people stopped. The bus driver was your dad. He took us in and drove us to the hospital despite all the protests from the people on the bus." He got up. "I'll always do whatever your dad asks. He is my best friend forever." He was about to leave, then he remembered something and laughed. "Remember," he said to her dad, "you were speeding, and the police stopped you in front of the hospital and asked you— why are you speeding? Why you are not on your route? And you know what he said?" He turned to Chloe, still laughing.

"No," said Chloe, "What?"

"He said..., he said," he could not talk because of his laughter. "He said—I got lost and was speeding back to my route." The nurse opened the door again, the doctor shook their hands and left.

"And what happened next?" asked Chloe. "Did the police believe you?"

"No," said her dad. "They took me to the police station where I told them the truth."

"Why didn't you tell the truth right away?"

"I didn't want Doctor Acosta to get in trouble. They would have started questioning him and I didn't want him to miss the birth of his child."

On the way to school, Chloe kept silent. She was thinking of Mr. Kimball and wondering what it was that had hurt him that much. He said something about a lie, but who lied to him and how? Then she realized that she'd also lied to her parents and to the doctor by not telling them about the drink. She wanted to be liked, she wanted to be a good party guest, which was why she had tried the tea. But now she was upset with herself for drinking it, and she really hated herself for agreeing to keep it a secret.

"What if I had the choice to be a good girl or to tell the truth? What should I do?"

Her dad answered after some thought. "I think you are a good girl, and you always tell the truth."

"Not always," said Chloe. And she added, "You didn't tell the truth to the police either."

"You are right," said her dad. "Sometimes to protect your friends you have to lie. Then you have to accept the consequences."

"What consequences did you accept?"

"Why do you think I am driving trucks and not buses?"

The rest of the drive, Chloe worked on rewriting her prepared presentation for her

Social Sciences class on the Golden Rule. Things had happened since the day before that made her rethink her main assumptions and conclusions.

The teacher of the Social Sciences class was Mr. Kimball; Chloe wondered if he'd be there or not.

When he brought her to school, her dad hugged Chloe and said, "Don't forget to take your pill. The next time is at 11am. It's very important."

"Ok," said Chloe.

"Do you have water?"

"Yes, Mom always gives me a bottle of water."

He hugged her goodbye, started to leave, then turned around and said, "You know I run the trucks on schedule. And I know that doing things on schedule is very important. Sometimes it's the difference between life and death." He smiled and added, "11am. Be a good girl."

I am low on blood sugar

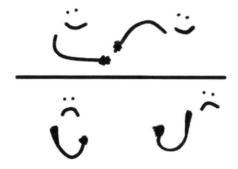

Golden Rule

Chloe had felt manipulated by Emma, but she blamed only herself for what happened. Yet when Emma tried to speak to her, Chloe avoided her. She saw that it made Emma nervous, but Chloe just couldn't talk to her.

The topic in her Social Sciences class was the Golden Rule. There was no sign that Mr. Kimball was distressed. He started the class by explaining to them that this rule was the cornerstone of religious and social morals around the world. "Treat others as *you* would like to be treated."

Q. Do you agree that you should treat others as you would like to be treated?

Yes. Sounds like a good moral rule of thumb.

No. It is one of those rules that sounds good, but when you give it some thought you can come up with many examples when it produces bad results. Can you think of such examples?

Mr. Kimball asked Chloe to start her presentation. She came to the front of the class with her notes. She started with, "I have problems with the Golden Rule."

Mr. Kimball interrupted her. "Please start with telling us whether you like the Golden Rule or not."

"I don't like it," said Chloe to the shock of the entire class.

Mr. Kimball said, "Let's take a quick survey. Who else doesn't like the Golden Rule, please raise your hand." No arm was raised.

"Now, if you do like the Golden Rule, please raise your arm now." Everybody raised their arms.

"Before we continue, who wants to give some examples of using the Golden Rule?"

He called on Emma, who was vigorously waving her hand.

"If I like something, I would offer that to my friend," said Emma looking significantly at Chloe. "Also, if somebody asks me to keep a secret, I'll keep it. And if I ask somebody to keep a secret, I expect them to do so."

"Interesting examples," said Mr. Kimball. "Please continue," he gestured to Chloe.

"I think there are three big problems with that rule."

"Really?" Mr. Kimball smiled to the class. "What are they?"

"First of all, why am I deciding how the other person wants to be treated? Who am I to decide what another person wants?"

"What do you mean?"

"Maybe the other person wants something different. Suppose I like tea," and she looked at Emma, "and the other person doesn't. Why should I be giving the other person tea? Why should I be insisting that the other person drinks tea if he doesn't like it? Only because I believe that he would do the same to me?"

"So what exactly is your complaint?"

"Why is the other person cut out of the decision process? The decision on how *he* should be treated? According to the Golden Rule, he has no say in it."

Q. Do you agree that you shouldn't be deciding how the other person is treated?

Yes. Of course, the other person knows better than anybody else how he wants to be treated.

No. It's perfectly all right for me to decide how to treat the other person by observing how he treats me. If I know that the other person is going to hit me, I should hit him. If I know that the other person is going to buy me a gift, I should buy him a gift.

"Ok," said Mr. Kimball, "let's see if you agree with this version of the Golden Rule." He wasn't smiling anymore. The class was very quiet. "You should treat others as *they* want to be treated."

Q. Do you agree that you should treat others as they want to be treated?

No. You are not a slave. Their wish is not your command.

51

Yes. In general, if it doesn't cause you any big problems, why not treat others as they want to be treated?

"No," said Chloe. "And here is the second problem with the rule."

"What is it?"

"I am not obliged to do something just because *they* wanted to."

"Ok," Mr. Kimball was a little irritated now. "What about this, a milder version of the Golden Rule: You should treat others as *they* want to be treated if *you* agree."

Q. Should you treat others as they want to be treated if you agree?

Yes. If you both agree to do something, there is no problem.

No. Even if both of you agreed, there still could be situations when you shouldn't be doing it. What if you agreed to rob a bank?

"Still no, and that brings me to the third problem," said Chloe.

"Why not?"

"Because other people could be involved in this treatment and they may not like it."

"What other people?"

"A third party."

"Can you give us an example?"

"What if I promised somebody to keep a secret, and they asked me to do that, so we both agreed," Chloe was looking again at Emma.

"So what's the problem?" asked Mr. Kimball.

"The problem is that there are other people from whom we are keeping the secret and those people would be very upset if they learned about it. So essentially I would be lying to those people."

Mr. Kimball was speechless. But he collected himself quickly. "Should you treat others as they want to be treated if you agree and there is no harm to anybody else? Would that be a good variation of the Golden Rule for you?"

Q. Should you treat others as they want to be treated if you agree and there is no harm to anybody else?

No. It should depend on the treatment.

Yes. Of course, why not?

"It's not much of a Golden Rule," said Chloe. "It's not much of a rule either, but the answer is still *no*."

"Why not?"

"What if I like ice cream, and the other person likes ice cream, and I buy that person ice cream, but he is overweight?"

"Well," said Mr. Kimball with a sigh, "If you don't like the Golden Rule, what rule would you suggest?"

She looked down, thinking. The class waited for her response.

"You should do good things and not do bad things."

"That is not a rule." Mr. Kimball was smiling to the class again. "What is good? What is bad? That is too general."

"No more general than the Golden Rule," said Chloe.

There was silence. Then Mr. Kimball said, "Ok, let's go with your rule: good, not bad." He looked directly at Chloe and asked, "Do you think lying is good or bad?"

"Of course, it's bad," she said.

"Is it really important to always tell the truth?"

"Of course, it is."

"Is it one of the most important things to do in your life?"

"Yes, it is."

"How do you know?"

Chloe was thinking. Mr. Kimball asked the class, "Why do we place such a premium on truth? Why is telling the truth one of the most important things in life?"

Q. Would you agree that telling the truth is the most important thing in your life?

Yes. People trust and respect you more when you tell the truth. And if you are a liar, other people will not want to deal with you regardless of all the virtues you might have and services you might offer. That's why telling the truth is the most important thing in your life. You wouldn't be able to put to good use whatever you think is more important if people simply don't believe you.

No. If you lie, you can achieve much more in life. If you lie, it's much easier to manipulate other people, to make them do what you want. And even if people catch you lying, you can just deny it. In the worst case, if your denial doesn't work, you can ask for forgiveness, and people will forgive you.

Nobody raised their hand to answer that question. Then Chloe thought of her parents, how she had lied to them and said, "Because when we lie, we hurt people."

"Exactly," said Mr. Kimball. "The worst pain we can cause other people is by lying."

He said, "Maybe I shouldn't be telling you this, but when a friend of mine found out that his parents were not his real parents, that they had adopted him as a baby, it was extremely painful for him."

He paused, then added, "I don't want to lie to you. It wasn't my friend. It was me. Do you know why it was painful?" The class was dead silent. "Not because I learned that they were not my parents. For me, they were wonderful parents. But because they didn't tell me that until now."

Chloe now understood what Mr. Kimball had been discussing with the doctor this morning. She said under her breath, "They wanted to protect you from pain."

But Mr. Kimball heard her. "I understand that. But they lied to me."

He then looked back at the entire class. "You know what point I am making?"

Again, nobody answered.

"We all agree—hope, all of us—that lying hurts. Lying is painful. But how do we know that? We don't feel the pain of other people. How do we know that lying hurts?"

"Because it hurts," said Chloe, not understanding where Mr. Kimball was going.

"Yes, it hurts *us*. But why do we not want to lie to others? How do we know it hurts *others*?"

And with Mr. Kimball nodding, Chloe breathed out, "Because of the Golden Rule."

School recess

During the next school recess, outside on the playground, Chloe checked the time on her phone. Exactly two minutes before 11am, she took out her pill and her bottle of water. Suddenly, Emma, who was playing hoops nearby with Jay, slipped and fell. Ms. Jones, the school's principal, ran over to her and then looked around. She noticed Chloe with her pill in one hand and an open bottle of water in another and yelled, "Give me that bottle!"

Chloe yelled back, "I need it!"

Ms. Jones, who was on her knees near Emma, yelled to Jay, "Bring me that bottle, quick!"

Jay started to run to Chloe. She saw that it was already one minute past 11am. She swallowed the pill and brought the bottle to her lips when Jay put his hand on the bottle.

Q. Should Chloe give her bottle to Jay?

No. It's her bottle and she needs it. That's being true to herself.

Yes. Emma needs it more, and urgently. Chloe being true to herself means making smart decisions, not hurtful ones.

Jay put his hand on the bottle, but Chloe pushed him away. Jay lost his balance and fell as Emma stood up and shouted, "I'm ok!"

In Ms. Jones' office

C hloe was sitting in the hall, waiting for her mom. She didn't know how her mom would react. She wasn't even sure whether what she did was right or wrong. Did she need the bottle more than Emma? How would she have known?

When her mom came, she hugged Chloe tightly and Chloe instantly understood that her mom knew and wasn't angry with her. A secretary led them to Ms. Jones' office. Ms. Jones recounted what had happened and said that because Chloe behaved so selfishly, she would be suspended from school for one day. Chloe was silent, but her mom told Ms. Jones that Chloe needed that bottle for her medicine. Ms. Jones said it didn't matter because Emma had needed it more.

"How do you know who needed it more?"

"I was there. I was in charge. It was my call."

Ms. Jones stood up, took out a few packages from her desk drawer, arranged them on a tray and went to a small aquarium that stood nearby on a small desk.

"I apologize. This is when I need to take care of my fish. Do you mind? It's a gift from my late grandmother." Obviously, Ms. Jones was trying to indicate nicely that the meeting was over.

But Chloe's mom wasn't ready to give up yet. "I don't mind," she said. "I understand that it's important to take care of living creatures at the right time. But you know what? Chloe needed this bottle at the right time as well. The doctor prescribed her pills and she had to take the pill right then with water. You didn't know that when you made your call, did you?"

With a small wooden spoon Mr. Jones took a little amount of mixture from each of her cartons and mixed them in a plastic container.

"We teach students the Golden Rule. Your daughter made a circus out of her Social Sciences class but that's another conversation. I hope you don't object to the Golden Rule, do you?"

"What does my objection have to do with this situation?"

"If your daughter were in Emma's place, you would've wanted her to get the bottle."

Ms. Jones was putting about half of her mixture from the container into the fish tank. The tank had gravel on the bottom, a few big stones, a couple of miniature bushes that looked like cactuses, and three brightly colored fish that circled around, opening their small mouths to catch their food. "You would beg her to give up the bottle. What if something bad happened to Emma because she didn't get water in time?"

"But what if something bad happened to Chloe if she had given the bottle away?"

"Chloe would've survived if she got water a few minutes later. Emma had just had an accident and needed the water urgently. You may disagree with me, but that decision was up to me, and I made it in the heat of the moment. Yes, I didn't have all the information. But even now, after what you told me, I feel it was the right choice." Ms.

Jones added the remaining mixture to the tank.

Her mom thought for a moment and then said, "You didn't ask for the bottle, you demanded it, right?"

"Yes, I demanded it."

"You even ordered somebody to take the bottle away, didn't you?"

"Yes, I told you I did. I am in charge and I made my decision."

"But the bottle was Chloe's property, wasn't it?"

"Yes, it was."

"So it wasn't up to you to decide whether to take the bottle or not. It wasn't *your* bottle."

"At that point, it didn't matter. Emma was in critical condition, I made the decision, and Chloe behaved selfishly. Besides, she hit Jay. Nobody used any force on Chloe, but she hit him." She took her tray with all the packages and brought it back to her desk.

Q. Should you defend your property by force?

No. At least, not always. If you use force, you can hurt somebody. Accidentally or not, you can even kill somebody. There is always risk to somebody's life when force is involved. And it's not worth creating that risk for the purpose of defending property. After all, property is not a person. Property is not even alive. Defending property with force and therefore putting somebody's life at risk can never be justified.

Yes. You should always defend your property with force. If your ownership of property is threatened, it means somebody initiated force against you. If they just use words, you can ignore them. But if they use force against you or against your property, yes, you should use force to defend yourself or your property. How else can you fight for what's yours? Don't feel ashamed for forcefully defending your property. Don't let them blame you, either. They started it.

"The bottom line—regardless of whose property it was—is that in my judgment a life was at risk and it was up to me to make the decision about the bottle."

As Chloe was watching the beautiful fish swimming near Ms. Jones' hand, her mom stood up, went to the aquarium, and took out a fish.

"I am low on blood sugar," she told Ms. Jones, who looked shocked. "If I don't eat, I could risk my life. I know this is your property, but my life is at risk and it is up to me to make the decision about the fish."

She brought the fish close to her mouth and pretended to take a bite. Then she threw the fish back into the tank.

Q. If Chloe's mom's life were really at risk, would it have given her the right to eat Ms. Jones' fish?

Yes. If this weren't a hypothetical question, she could have died if she didn't eat the fish.

No. It was not her fish. If she really had such an unusual, life-threatening condition, she should have thought about it in advance and should have taken appropriate measures, like bringing some food with her. She didn't do that, so it's her problem and she shouldn't have the right to solve her problem by destroying other people's property.

Mr. Gerick, Ms. Jones' secretary, rushed into the office and stood next to Ms. Jones. Barely hiding her anger, Ms. Jones said slowly, "The suspension goes on Chloe's permanent record. She is not going to be accepted into any good college. Mr. Gerick, please show them out."

Her mom took Chloe's hand and they left.

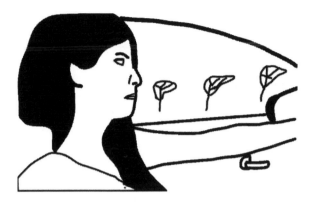

In the car with Mom

In the car, Chloe's mom called her dad and asked him to meet them. She was shaking her head, talking to herself while driving.

"What is the definition of property?" asked Chloe. She wanted to calm her mom down, but she also sincerely wanted to understand this argument.

"Property is just stuff."

"Any stuff?"

"Any."

"You said that the bottle was *my* property? Why?"

"Because in general, property is the stuff that belongs to somebody. What's yours is yours. And nobody should take your property from you without your permission."

Q. Is it true nobody should take your property from you without your permission?

Yes. It's yours.

No. There may be situations when your property is needed to save the lives of other people.

Her dad was waiting for them outside his truck at a highway exit. He came to the car window.

"Chloe didn't give her bottle of water to another girl who fell on the ground while playing basketball. Chloe needed the bottle to take her medicine, like you told me," her mom said. "She got suspended for one day. Dr. Acosta is your friend. Please call him and ask him to write a note saying that Chloe needed the bottle or she could've died."

"How can I do that? Is it true? Do you really believe she could have died if she took her medicine a few minutes later?"

"That's not important. The suspension will stay on her record and it'll be harder for Chloe to get into college."

Q. If her dad knows that the doctor will write the note if asked, should he ask him?

No. He believes he would be asking his friend to lie.

Yes. This is very important for Chloe. If she doesn't get the note, the suspension will be on her record, she may not be accepted to college, and her entire life could be ruined.

After her dad refused to call the doctor, Chloe's mom took the car on a road that wasn't the shortest way home.

"Where are we going?" Chloe asked.

"We are going to see Dr. Acosta. I'll ask him to write the note."

Q. Should Chloe ask her mom not to go to the doctor to ask for a note?

Yes. That note would be a lie.

No. Lie or no lie, Chloe needs that note badly.

"Mom, I don't want you to go to the doctor. I don't want the note," said Chloe.

Mom shrugged and turned the car toward home.

"I did what I was told to do. Was I a bad girl?" asked Chloe.

"You did what you should have done."

"But what if Emma had died because I didn't give her the bottle?"

"What if you had died? You know it was important for you to take that pill."

"Ms. Jones told me I was selfish because I was thinking of myself first."

"You should always think of yourself first."

Q. Should you always think of yourself first?

Yes. Who else would be thinking of you besides you?

No. It should depend on the situation. If other people are in greater danger than you, you should think of them first. And if it is your child, a close relative, or a close friend, you should think of them first even if you are in greater danger.

You are so goody-goody

Invitation

Then her mom added, "You should call Emma tonight."

"What should I say?"

"You should apologize."

Q. Should Chloe apologize to Emma?

No. Because that would be a lie if she didn't feel that she did something wrong— and she didn't. Emma also would know that the apology was not sincere and would think badly of Chloe.

Yes. Even if someone is not responsible for bad things happening to the other person, sometimes it's good to show compassion and to say sorry.

"I won't call her," said Chloe.

They arrived at the house. Her mom turned the engine off in the garage and took out her phone.

"Hi, Ms. Benson, this is Chloe's mom. Can I please speak to Emma?"

Chloe was shaking her head *no* but didn't say anything.

"Emma, this is Chloe's mom. She got a suspension. Yes. Suspension for one day. Because she didn't give you her bottle of water. Yes, it's terrible, but that's not all. Ms. Jones is saying that it will go on her record. Yes, it means she will not be accepted to good colleges. No, you don't have to be sorry. Chloe apologizes to you."

"Mom," yelled Chloe, but her mom just waved her away.

"Can you please write a note that you were ok, that you didn't need the water? Maybe it'll change Ms. Jones' mind."

She listened and then gave her phone to Chloe.

"Chloe," said Emma "Why don't you come over in two hours and we talk about it?"

"Ok," said Chloe.

Conversation with Emma

Two hours later, Chloe's mom drove her to Emma's house. When Emma met Chloe at the door, she pointed to the note attached to the door from the inside and said, "Read it." The note said: *Don't open the door, even if the police call. Only I can open it. Emma.*

"Got it?" she asked.

"Got it," answered Chloe.

The music was as loud as during the last party. In the living room, a group of teenagers were drinking and eating. A few couples were slow dancing.

Emma led her to the kitchen. A few people who were there left with drinks in their hands. Almost immediately, Kevin came in and picked up a bottle of beer from the refrigerator.

"Hi Chloe." He greeted her with a friendly smile. Emma apparently didn't tell him about the latest complications at school. "Did you like the tea?"

"It was ok," Chloe said and smiled back. *Why do I keep lying?*

"Would you like more?"

"No, thank you."

"Why are you here?" asked Emma. Kevin left, and they were alone.

"I want to apologize."

"You don't mean it."

"I am sorry if I upset you."

"This isn't an apology. It's a lie. Why are you doing it? Because you need a note from me?"

"No," said Chloe. "Because my mom told me I should."

"If you repeat somebody's words as yours and don't mean it, it's a lie, isn't it?"

Q. Is saying what you don't mean always a lie?

No. It's ok to sometimes say what you don't really mean. If nobody gets hurt by it, it is a white lie exception.

Yes. Chloe would benefit from pretending to care. A white lie exception cannot be applied here.

"Yes, I agree," said Chloe. Whatever happened, she had had enough of lying. "It might have been the wrong decision, but it was my property and I didn't have to give you my bottle. I have nothing to apologize for."

Her cell rang. It was her mom.

"Chloe, is everything ok?"

"Yes."

"I have to go to work." Chloe's mother worked in a theater and often had performances at night. "If Emma's parents can drive you home, I'd appreciate that. But if they can't, call Dad to pick you up."

And then she asked, "Are Emma's parents there?"

Q. Chloe didn't know for sure whether Emma's parents were there or not. Is it ok for her to say that Emma's parents are there?

No. This information is important to her mom. If Chloe answers "Yes," it's a lie.

Yes. It's ok. She didn't want to inconvenience her mom. It's not a big deal. And she didn't know—Emma's parents could be there.

"Yes," whispered Chloe.

"What did you say?"

"Yes."

"Can I talk to them?"

"They are not right here."

Q. Can a true statement be a lie?

Yes. Obviously, it's a continuation of the lie that the parents are there.

No. Again, not a big deal. And of course, it is true, because Emma's parents are not right there.

Chloe hung up and looked at Emma who apparently had been listening.

"Would you like some pizza?" Emma pointed at some open pizza boxes left on the table.

"No, thank you."

Emma stood up and got a box of chocolate gelato ice cream from the refrigerator.

"Ice cream?"

"No, thanks."

Kevin came back to the kitchen, opened a bottle of wine, poured a glass, smiled, and left.

"Some wine, maybe?" asked Emma, pouring wine into two glasses.

"No, thank you."

"Why not?"

"I don't like it."

"How do you know you don't like it if you don't try it?"

"I am not an alcoholic and I don't want to become one."

"You are not an alcoholic and you can always drop it if you don't like it. Try a sip."

Q. Should Chloe try a sip of wine?

No. It's illegal.

Yes. One sip is not a big deal.

"No," said Chloe. "I still have a headache from that tea you gave me."

Emma lit a cigarette and offered it to Chloe. "Have a smoke."

"No, thanks."

"Why not?"

"Give it to me." Chloe took the cigarette and tossed it into the sink.

"What are you doing?"

"You enjoy smoking it. I enjoy destroying it."

"You are afraid of your parents, aren't you?"

"No, I'm not afraid."

"They don't need to know."

"No, I'm not smoking."

"Not cool. Take a smoke."

"No."

"Ok, here's my offer. I'll write you a note that I didn't need the water if you smoke a cigarette or drink a glass of wine."

"No."

"My final offer: half of a cigarette, or half of a glass of wine."

"Emma, why are you doing this?" Chloe got up. "You call yourself my friend, you heard me say *no,* and you are still pushing me. Why?"

"I'll tell you why." Emma put the cigarette into an empty pizza box and poured wine from her glass on top of it to extinguish the light. "You are so goody-goody. Teachers say you are good. My mother says you are good. Jay is saying you are always telling the truth. But you are no better than me. You didn't share your precious water when they told you I might die. You lied that you wanted to apologize. You lied that my parents are here—I heard you! You are not better than me, you just pretend that you care. You pretend that you tell the truth. You are a phony. A fake."

Emma started crying. Chloe went to hug her. "I am sorry, Emma. I am really sorry." She started crying too.

Q. Is it a lie to say "I am sorry" even if you don't think you did anything wrong?

Yes. It's a lie. "I am sorry" normally means you are apologizing. Chloe could have said "Please don't cry," or "I understand how you feel," instead of saying something that looks like and could be interpreted as a lie.

No. "I am sorry" doesn't always means that a person is apologizing. Often it expresses compassion and empathy. It was perfectly appropriate for Chloe to say "I am sorry" in this situation.

"No! I don't need your *sorry*." Emma pushed her away. "I don't want you around anymore. Please leave."

Chloe turned and ran out of the house.

Jump in

Chloe walked briskly for a few minutes to calm down. She could have easily walked all the way home, but it was getting late and she decided to call her dad to pick her up. As her mom said, he would be expecting her call. Suddenly, a car stopped in front of her.

It was Kevin. He said Emma sent him to give her a ride. "Get in." But Chloe hesitated. He looked pleasant and sober, but she remembered that he had had some wine.

"Jump in," he said, smiling.

Q. Should Chloe get in the car with Kevin? Would you get in if you were in her place?

No. It would be safer to call her dad for a ride.

Yes. It wasn't far away and he didn't appear drunk.

"No, thank you," said Chloe.

"I have a note from Emma. Get in, and I'll give it to you."

Q. Should Chloe get in?

Yes. This note is important. It is possible that Kevin might give her the note even if she refused the ride. But it's more likely that he wouldn't and Chloe may regret that for the rest of her life. What's the risk? He did drink some wine, but he appeared completely sober and it was only a few minutes' drive. What could go wrong?

In any decision, there are some pros and cons. Here, agreeing to get into the car and getting the note is clearly better than risking not getting into any college.

No. If Chloe gets into the car with Kevin, she will be lying to her mom by not taking a ride with her dad. Not to mention that she will be risking her life.

Chloe hesitated. Kevin got out and went around to open the passenger door.

"At your service, ma'am!"

Chloe laughed and got in.

The runner

They drove a few blocks before Kevin said, "Would you like to come to my place first?"

"No," answered Chloe right away.

"Come on. We can listen to music. I have a great selection. We can drink some coffee. Or tea."

The word "tea" alarmed Chloe. She now regretted getting into the car.

"Stop the car. I want to get out. "

"I was joking. I'll take you straight home. Don't worry."

"Please, stop the car."

"Here's your note." He had no intention of stopping. He tried to get the note from his pocket but his seatbelt was in the way. He unbuckled himself, took out the note, and handed it to Chloe. He took his eyes off the road to do that and Chloe saw that the car was about to hit three old men who were slowly crossing the road. The middle one was in a wheelchair.

She screamed, "Kevin!" and took the steering wheel to turn it away. She saw that if she did that, the car might hit a woman running on the sidewalk, who was wearing a reflective yellow vest.

Q. Should she turn the steering wheel?

Yes. One person might be killed, but if she does nothing, three people may be killed. If your answer is "No," how would you answer if it weren't three people but a thousand? A million?

No. It's not her right and not her responsibility to decide who lives and who dies. The argument that if Chloe doesn't turn the steering wheel, then she would have killed three old men is invalid. She wouldn't be responsible for their deaths. Kevin would.

Kevin tried to take control back, but the car turned and hit the woman.

"No!" screamed Chloe. Kevin turned the car from the sidewalk and back onto the road.

"Stop!" yelled Chloe, but Kevin kept driving. Chloe looked back at the runner, who lay sprawled. Chloe pulled her door handle and the door opened.

Q. Should Chloe jump out of the car?

No. She would only hurt herself. She could die from her jump. It's not her obligation to help the woman.

Yes. Obviously, she estimated that she had a good chance to survive the jump and that she may be able to help the woman.

Chloe didn't know how long she was out, but once she regained consciousness, she saw she was not far from the woman. She could not get up or feel her legs, so she crawled closer. The woman appeared to be dead, but when Chloe touched her arm, she opened her eyes and looked at Chloe. She slowly took off her tiara and put it on Chloe's head.

Then she whispered, "Don't take it off. Wear it all the time." A small stream of blood started dripping from her mouth. "It's not your fault" was the last thing Chloe heard.

Flying Fox

"Chloe?"

Chloe was lying in a bed. Her head hurt badly and it was hard to collect her thoughts. Images flowed through her mind: three old men slowly crossing the road, one in a wheelchair, two others each holding a handle of that wheelchair, all three wearing black suits and black hats. All looking straight at Chloe with panic in their eyes. Suddenly, from the side, a yellow running vest hit her with a burst of light.

"Chloe?"

She opened her eyes. The room was dark, but some light came from the hall through the opened door. She noticed a shadow, yellow and black.

"Did you call me?" she asked.

"Yes." The shadow moved closer. It was a strange animal, covered with golden fur and with black wings that looked like arms crisscrossed in front of it.

"Who are you?"

"I am Adriel."

It made sense. The Giant Golden Flying Fox. Yes, with a burst of clarity, Chloe remembered the discussion with her dad. What was its fancy Latin name? Jubatus. Acerodon jubatus.

"Where did you come from?"

"From Paraten."

The animal looked a little like a fox, but was standing and the wings indicated it could fly. Its head, with long ears and a long nose, looked like a fox's head. And the animal was certainly golden—especially its fur behind his head, like a scarf. Mainly golden, but also some black and brown and grey gave it a slight shine, reflecting the dim light from the door. "What are you doing here?"

"I came to take you with me."

"Where do you want to take me?"

"To just prince."

That sounded strange. Did the fox have a problem with the prince? Or did it want to put Chloe in her place? After all, it was just a prince—not a king or a queen. But the tone was respectful, and Chloe decided to let it go. For now.

"Why?"

"To take a test."

"What test?"

"To become a Truth Seeker."

"What do Truth Seekers do?"

"Seek the truth." The fox tapped its long, thin fingers on its chest, as if trying to calm itself. That's when Chloe noticed that it had a big crystal in one paw and a thin flat snake in the other. The snake was pink with a repeating pattern of green diamonds. Strangely, Chloe didn't feel afraid.

"Why should I do it?"

"You'll help just prince and his people."

"Who is this prince?"

"He is just prince."

"Why can't you ask somebody else to do this?"

"There is nobody else. You caused the death of the Truth Seeker. You must replace the Truth Seeker."

That was too painful for Chloe. *"Did I kill somebody?"* But she couldn't finish her thought. Suddenly she became very tired.

"Leave me alone. I am not going anywhere."

"Why are you so rude?"

"I am not rude. I am tired."

"Please tell me why you are not going. What should I tell just prince?"

"I don't go to unknown places with unknown people." She realized this wasn't "people," so she quickly added, "With unknown persons." She still wasn't sure that she could call this creature a "person," but the Golden Fox ignored her linguistic struggle and said, "Do you always go only where you are allowed to go?"

"We've just met. I don't know you."

"What does it mean to know somebody? I told you my name is Adriel." The fox was becoming impatient.

"Are you a girl or a boy?" asked Chloe.

"I am a girl. How is that important?" The Golden Fox tapped herself again with her long nails. The snake raised its head and looked at Chloe with vertical pupils. "Do you know me now? Will you please get up and come with me?"

Chloe wasn't sure that this conversation was really happening. Her head was cloudy. Her eyes were heavy. Yet she decided to give this request a thought.

Q. Should Chloe agree to go with the Golden Fox?

Yes. It's her life, and if she wants to be true to herself, she should be able to explore interesting opportunities. This seems to be an interesting opportunity. There may be some risks involved, but the opportunity is unique and exciting and may never be presented again.

No. She shouldn't go. It may be a lie or a trap. It could be a hallucination. She is sick after the accident and she may go to a place where she could get hurt.

"No, I am not going." Chloe closed her eyes and went to sleep.

When she opened her eyes, Adriel was there again.

"I spoke to just prince. He has a message for you. The message consists of five points. Point one is an offer: Would you like to start the test without going anywhere? Point two is an option: You have until tonight to decide whether you want to be the Truth Seeker or not. Point three is a warning: If you don't start your test now, you will lose your chance and may regret it later. Point four is a guarantee: You are safe during the test; nothing bad will happen to you. Point five is an appeal: He needs you."

"What kind of test?"

"I'll ask you a question. You have the whole day to think how to answer it. If your answer is correct, you can decide whether you want to continue with the test or not. It will be up to you."

"You said I would have to go somewhere? Now you are saying I don't?"

"I'll come back tomorrow. If you decide to go to just prince, I'll take you and you will deliver him the answer."

"I am not sure. I have many more questions, but I am really tired."

She heard some muffled steps and voices from the hall. Adriel probably heard it too.

"If you decide to go, just prince will answer all your questions. I can't tell you anything more. And I am sorry, but my time is up and I will have to leave you in a minute."

Chloe sighed heavily. "What's the question?"

"What's your most important job?"

"I am not working yet," said Chloe, not understanding where the conversation was going.

Silence. Chloe raised her head a little. "What about the test?"

"This is the question of the test," said Adriel.

"I am sorry, what is?"

"What's your most important job?"

"But I am not working yet," said Chloe. "I am not an adult yet."

"I mean what is your main responsibility in life? What is the most important thing you should be concerned about? If you are allowed to focus on only one thing, what is it?"

"Excuse me," Chloe tried again, "but what do Truth Seekers do?"

The fox gave the same answer, "Seek the truth." She started opening her wings to fly away.

Trying to learn something about the question, Chloe asked, "When you say your job, do you mean me or anybody?"

"Both," said the fox, and then she disappeared.

It rains in my heart

Parents visiting

When Chloe woke up, she was thinking about the question.

"What is the most important thing you should be concerned about?" was one of the clarifications that the fox gave.

"The most important thing? What is the most important thing... and what is the most important thing that I have?" Chloe really liked the sneakers that her mom had just bought for her. She loved her pink leotard that she wore in her ballet classes—when she'd put it on, it would change her completely, and she liked how she looked. She loved her new basketball that her dad had just bought for her. It smelled great. She played with an old one, but she took the new one to bed. But that would be a ridiculous answer to Adriel's question, wouldn't it? When she met the flying fox again, how could she say that the most important thing in her life was her basketball? Or leotard? Or sneakers? Ridiculous.

The door opened slowly and a nurse let her crying mom and concerned dad into the room. Chloe smiled and they smiled back, happily surprised that Chloe was awake and relatively ok. But then Chloe remembered...

It's not that she hadn't remembered it before, but it was stored far back in her brain. Seeing her parents, Chloe clearly recalled Kevin handing her the note, the old men in black hats, and the woman runner!

Chloe started to cry. "What happened to the woman?"

"The doctor said we shouldn't discuss the accident with you." Her mom was crying too.

Q. If the doctor said not to discuss the accident with Chloe, is it ok for her mom to answer her questions?

No. The doctor knows better than her. If Chloe's mom cares about Chloe's health, she shouldn't answer her questions about the accident.

Yes. Her mom knows Chloe better than any doctor. It's ultimately her decision what to tell Chloe.

"Is Kevin ok?"

Dad stepped forward. "The police told us not to discuss the accident with you."

Q. If the police said not to discuss the accident with Chloe, is it ok for her mom to answer her questions?

Yes. If her mom feels that Chloe's recovery depends on this information and that Chloe will suffer greatly not knowing what happened (which could result in deteriorating physical or mental health), then her mom should tell Chloe what Chloe wants to know.

No. If she does that, she is interfering with a police investigation, which could be illegal. The concern about Chloe's health is irrelevant and invalid. There is no way that Chloe would die or substantially change her recovery because of knowing or not knowing some facts that happened after the accident.

"Is Kevin ok?"

Her dad stepped forward. "The police told us not to discuss the accident with you."

Her mom nodded "yes" behind him. She looked around and tried to smile. "They told us you'd be ok. This is a good hospital."

"It looks all right," said Chloe.

"I know it's good because Uncle Adam is in here and he is getting good care."

"Mom," Chloe asked again, "is Kevin all right?"

"Yes," said her mom. "He is being held by the police, but he will be home soon."

"Is the woman...the runner?" asked Chloe, almost whispering.

Her mom lowered her head and her dad said, "We should not discuss it."

Chloe started crying again. Her mom said, "Maybe she is alive. Maybe she is just in a coma."

Her dad came closer. "Where did you get this?" He carefully touched the tiara.

"Please don't touch it," asked Chloe.

He looked at Chloe, read something in her eyes, and understood that he shouldn't ask any more questions. He took out his phone, took a picture, and showed it to Chloe. The base was a thin, silver circle covered with blue stones. All of them were of equal size, except one in the center that was long and looked like an eye.

"The stones are called sapphires," said her dad. He did a quick search on his phone. "According to Hebrew history, King Solomon and Abraham wore talismans of sapphire. It is said that the Law given to Moses at Mount Sinai was engraved on tablets of sapphire. This stone is a symbol of power and wise judgment."

She looked at the picture and noticed something written in cursive, burned in the base. She read it aloud. "Veritas Liberabit Vos"

Her father checked his cell again. "That's Latin. It means: Truth shall set you free."

Q. Can truth set a person free?

No. A person can be free or not regardless of whether he is telling the truth or not. A criminal in cuffs is not free even if he is telling the truth.

Yes. If a person lies, he is controlled by the lies and becomes a slave of the lies. He has to remember what he lied about and to whom. If a person is telling the truth, he is not afraid of consequences, anything, and anybody. He is truly free.

Her dad said, "I know a thing or two about jewelry. This is precious. And I think it'll protect you."

Chloe immediately thought that this tiara was the right answer. It certainly became the most valued thing that Chloe ever had. And it wasn't ridiculous.

Q. Is the tiara the most important thing in Chloe's life?

No. It's just a thing. It could be lost or destroyed. And some other thing could become more valuable.

Yes. It's certainly the most expensive. Also it might protect Chloe, so it has additional value. And even if something else becomes more valuable later, it wouldn't change the fact that right now this is the most important thing.

On the other hand, Chloe thought, maybe something else was even more precious. Such as the car that her dad had bought. Or maybe their house. Yes, that's it. The house. She wondered what cost more, the tiara or the house. And then she thought that the answer should be more general. It's money.

Q. Is money the most important thing in your life?

Yes. If you have enough money, you can buy anything. You can buy any necklace. You can buy any car. You can buy any house.

No. There are things that money can't buy. Can you name some?

Then Chloe asked, "Mom, what's the most important thing for you?"

Her mom, who was quiet all this time and listening intensely to their conversation about the tiara, said, "You." She turned to Chloe's dad and smiled. "I am sorry. My family." He smiled and nodded in agreement.

Q. Is family the most important thing in your life?

Yes. Your family loves you and supports you unconditionally. Family members love you regardless of what you do, regardless of whether you are a good or a bad person. And you should support them back. If you don't have even your family behind you, then nobody will support you. And if nobody supports you, you won't achieve anything in life.

No. What if you don't have a family? Or what if you have a strong disagreement or bad relations with your family? Is that the end of your life?

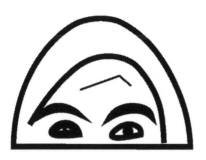

Two questions

After her parents left, Chloe tried to sleep but was unceremoniously interrupted by doctors and nurses that came and went. At one point, a policeman tried to talk to her but was refused by the doctor.

All this time, she knew that she had to answer two related questions and she tried to concentrate whenever she could. The questions were: "What's the most important job?" and "Should I go with the flying fox when she comes for me?"

She felt miserable. It wasn't a specific physical pain, just a cloudy mind. It was hard to focus, and that was frustrating. Did she kill a person? The runner? Was she a murderer? A murderess? Did she kill somebody else? What did the fox say? That she killed a Truth Seeker? *What on Earth is that Truth Seeking business? What do I have to do with anything like that? Did I have a choice? Did I have to take the steering wheel? Couldn't I turn it so that nobody would be killed?*

Mom said that maybe the runner in the yellow vest was in a coma. Does that mean I didn't kill her? Or didn't kill her yet? Or was Mom just making it up to calm me down?

On top of all that, Chloe was extremely upset with herself for lying. She knew that she lied to her mom when she implied that Emma's parents were present at the party.

She lied to herself when she drank the mysterious tea. And she lied to herself when she got into the car with Kevin. And of course, she lied to her parents because she didn't tell them about that. And she didn't tell them about the tea either. She was a liar. And she was a murderess.

She should not go with the fox. She had already gotten into a car when she knew she shouldn't have. And forget about the question about the most important job—if she was not going, she didn't have to answer it.

Should she ask her parents? She might as well decide not to go. There was no way her dad or her mom would approve. If she wasn't going, should she tell her parents anyway? That was another question she'd think about later. She had to concentrate on these two questions.

Was there any other problem with not telling her parents except that they would be against it? This was not a secret. Or was it? The fox never actually asked her to keep it a secret. But she felt that if she told anybody about it, it might ruin the whole thing and she might not be able to go.

Kevin also didn't ask her to keep it a secret when he offered "the tea." But Emma did. And Chloe knew that it was a secret right away—the way they behaved, looking around, lowering their voices. The same way she knew that drinking alcohol at the party was a secret. And look at the disasters it caused. She got sick from "the tea," and she killed somebody after Kevin got drunk.

What would happen if she went with the fox? What was the worst that could happen? Would she kill someone else? Would she die?

What was the worst that could happen if she didn't go? Nothing. Exactly. Nothing. Would she ever regret it? Would she ever get a chance like that? Would she live the rest of her life asking *why didn't I go?*

Was she just selfish, like Ms. Jones said? Was she thinking of just herself? Was it just the curiosity of the unknown that excited her? Well, the fox sounded serious. It seemed *they,* whoever they were, really needed her.

If only she could ask somebody to make the decision for her. If only she trusted and believed that anybody in the world could choose for her. No, it was her job.

Nurse

After lunch, a man wearing a white robe and round cap came in. He looked very young, almost like a teenager, maybe because of his small height, rosy cheeks, and springy walk. But his mustache and constant friendly and wise smile gave away his real age of about thirty.

"Hi, Chloe," he said. "My name is Arif. I am your nurse for today."

"Nice name," said Chloe.

"Thank you. It means *knowing* in Urdu, which is the language in Pakistan."

"Is that cap from Pakistan? Nice!" Chloe tried to be friendly, but once she asked that question, she realized that it might not have been appropriate. Maybe a little too personal, maybe a little condescending.

But Arif didn't mind. "Yes. I am a Pakistani," He gently corrected her. "But it is a Muslim cap and I bought it here. It is called a *taqiyah*."

They were quiet for a moment. With a smile, but in a serious tone, he said, "According to hospital regulations, jewelry is not allowed, and I must ask you to take off your head crown."

"It's not a crown," said Chloe. "It's a tiara. And I don't want to take it off."

"This regulation is needed because jewelry is often a habitat for viruses and bacteria," he explained. "Jewelry could also interfere with some medical procedures such as X-rays."

"I can't take it off. I need to wear it all the time." She saw that he wasn't convinced and rushed to add, "It's a very special gift. From a very special person."

"Even more reason to take it off. Jewelry could be lost or broken. The hospital cannot assume any responsibility if that happens."

"If I take it off, I will die."

"Why would you die?"

"Please don't make me take it off. If I take it off, I'll die."

Q. Was it ok for Chloe to lie?

Yes. Of course. It was important for her to keep the tiara on. How else could she convince Arif to leave her alone? He wouldn't believe that she'd die, so it was not really a lie. She was giving him an excuse to make an exception to hospital regulations. Arif represents the hospital and Chloe is kind of a hostage there. She can't leave the hospital, so she has to do whatever they tell her? She can't take the tiara off. Where would she go if they throw her out from the hospital?

No. It was not ok. Arif wouldn't think that she'd die if she took the tiara off, but he was probably convinced that *Chloe thought* that she would die. She obviously didn't think that, so it was a lie. While people sometimes benefit from their lies, it doesn't mean that they should lie. She should have told the truth; if that didn't work, she should have accepted any consequences. Either choice, taking off the tiara or leaving the hospital is better than lying. She lost a part of herself. She is not a truthful person to the degree she was before she made this lie.

Arif kept a trace of his smile, but went silent for a moment. Then he said, "Wait here, I'll be right back." He came back in a few minutes with a plastic package. He opened it up and took out a cap made from elastic cloth, a headscarf. It was black with a dark red band encircling the base. A tie in the back looked like another, smaller hat with a special space for a pony tail.

"Try that."

She put it on and checked it on her cell in mirror mode. The headscarf looked beautiful and covered her tiara completely.

"Thank you," said Chloe. "Let me pay for it, please."

"Don't worry, it cost almost nothing."

"Am I allowed to wear this? Here, in the hospital?"

"Yes. If you tell them that you are thinking of becoming a Muslim and this is your hijab, a part of your religious dress code."

Q. Should Chloe agree to lie about her religion?

No. Pretending to belong to a certain religion to accommodate personal conveniences is too much. This is disgusting.

Yes. She doesn't have to go to a mosque. She doesn't have to pray on the Koran. This is not a big deal. This is just a headscarf. Sometimes to achieve their goals, people have to play certain roles. It can't be that bad; everybody does that one time or another. There are no exceptions. Also, if somebody attacks you, not by words, but by physical force, you are entitled to defend yourself with force. And when you are entitled to use force, you are certainly entitled to lie. In this case, the hospital attacked Chloe. If she doesn't take the tiara off, she will be thrown out. Even if she finds another hospital that will let her keep the tiara, it might take a long time and she will likely suffer physical harm. The hospital could be justified if this regulation was for everybody without any exceptions. But they did make an exception for religious groups. If it's ok to let Muslims keep their jewelry on under headscarves, it should be ok for everybody else.

"Thanks," said Chloe. "I'll do that."

"Remember that you have to wear it in the presence of adult males who are not part of your immediate family." Now they were both smiling.

"You can hide your tiara under that headscarf in high school too. Are you still in high school?" he asked.

"Yes. Are you in college?"

"Yes. I am studying medicine and journalism."

"Arif, what's your main goal in life?"

"I want to change the world," he said. "I want the world to become a better place."

"What if you can't change the world? Your life would be wasted?"

"No," said Arif, smiling. "Even if I make a small change in the world, I'll be happy."

Chloe smiled back.

"Even if I make somebody smile, I am changing the world a little," said Arif, and they both smiled again.

Q. Should your most important purpose in life be to change the world?

No. What if you are happy with the world you were born into? What if you are happy with your country, your people, and your family? Then your life has no purpose and no sense?

Yes. If you leave the world exactly the same as you came in, what was the point of you being born? What difference did it make? None.

"Arif," said Chloe, "could you help me visit my uncle? He is somewhere in this hospital."

"Well," said Arif, hesitantly, "you are not allowed to leave the room."

"This is your chance to change the world, Arif," said Chloe, smiling.

"Your tiara is beautiful," said Arif, smiling back. "I knew you liked it a lot. Even when you were unconscious, you would not let us take it off."

"I told you, this is a gift from a special person," said Chloe, apologetically.

"Can you keep a secret?"

Here we go again, thought Chloe. She said, "Yes."

"This is what I can do for you," said Arif. "I'll find and tell you where your uncle is. I'll help you disconnect from the IV. I'll help you move to the wheelchair. And I'll check when nobody is around your room. Then you'll be on your own, ok?"

Uncle Adam's request

Chloe didn't have to travel far to visit Uncle Adam. He was in the adjacent wing, two floors below. She almost convinced herself that "change the world" was the right answer, but knowing that her uncle was a famous, brilliant mathematician, she wanted to check if this answer withstood his scientific scrutiny.

She found him in bed, pale and sweaty. He had a mask on his face and many wires attached to his body from a grey metal box with a red button located near the window. On his nightstand, there was a pen, graph paper, and some mathematical books. After greeting him, Chloe asked how he felt. He didn't answer directly. He said, "I know about your accident. You look good. You can move around." It was hard to hear him because he was talking softly through the mask.

"Uncle Adam, you don't look well."

"Please talk louder. I can't hear well."

"You look well, Uncle Adam," said Chloe much louder. What came out was different than how she started, but she felt that in this situation a little white lie is appropriate.

"What's that on your head," he asked. "Did you become Muslim?"

Q. Should Chloe tell Uncle Adam the true reason why she was wearing the headscarf?

Yes. She shouldn't lie. If she doesn't want to tell everything, she can say that she doesn't want to answer that question.

No. It's another little white lie. Is information very important to him? No. Is Chloe under any obligation to give him that information? No. If she says she doesn't want to answer this question, it would sound a little rude. She can achieve the same goal with a nicer wording.

"No, Uncle Adam, just fooling around. I like wearing it."

"Finding little joys in life?"

"Sure, why not?" She smiled and pointed to her wheelchair. "Right time to enjoy life."

He hesitated, then said, "I am tired. I want to end it all."

"Why, Uncle Adam?" Chloe was in shock.

"Wrong question." He smiled drily. "Give me one reason why people should want to live."

Without much thinking, Chloe said what she had on her mind. "Well, to make a change in the world."

"What?"

"To change the world," she was almost screaming now.

"And that is a good reason for everybody?"

"Yes," Chloe couldn't back out now. Besides, at this point, she truly believed in it.

"It doesn't work."

"Why?"

"That it's an incomplete reason to live."

"What do you mean, incomplete?"

"It's inadequate. It can't be applied to all people."

"Why not?"

"What if a person doesn't change the world?"

"Then what?"

"Then according to your theory, he shouldn't want to live, right?"

"Well," Chloe used Arif's argument, "anybody can change the world a little."

Now, it was his turn to ask, "What do you mean, a little?"

Arif had just answered that, it made sense and was funny when he said it, so Chloe said, "If a person makes another person smile," and smiled. Uncle Adam didn't smile back, so Chloe tried again. "Suppose somebody just wrote a 'thank you' note, or in some other way just created a pleasant memory for somebody else, this person is already changing the world."

"Changing the world," repeated Uncle Adam. Then he continued slowly, "You are really stretching the concept of changing the world. Anyway, this is still incomplete. What if the person is alone, doesn't have any friends, or relatives, reading books in some closet? According to you, he shouldn't live, right?" He breathed heavily, then added, "He can't do a little thing for somebody else, because there is nobody else around."

Uncle Adam closed his eyes and continued as if he wasn't arguing with Chloe but talking to himself. It was hard to hear him. Chloe moved closer.

"Anyway, the entire notion of changing the world is questionable. It makes too many assumptions, which are not necessarily true or even reasonable. What if the world doesn't want to be changed? And most importantly, who decides what the world wants? 99% of all people? 51% of all people? Or some exploited minority? And who decides what the world is? A family? A country? A city? The Earth? The Universe? Also, who decides what good change is? You are talking about good change only, aren't you? Is it up to the person to decide whether he is making good change, or does it presume some societal judgment, some death panel, deciding somebody has a right to live because he is changing the world in a good way and somebody else isn't?"

There was silence. Then Uncle Adam opened his eyes and looked at Chloe.

"Ok, Uncle Adam. You convinced me. What is the right answer then?"

"The right answer to what question?"

"What's the most important thing in life to do?"

"I don't know." He added, "But at least I helped you to eliminate one answer, didn't I?"

"Yes, you did."

"You appreciate it, don't you?"

"Yes, I do."

Uncle Adam breathed quietly under the mask for a minute. He closed his eyes.

"Will you do something for me then?"

"Yes, sure, what is it?"

"Do you see the red button on the side of this grey box?" He opened his eyes and pointed to the metal box near the window.

"Yes?"

"Press it."

"And what will happen then?"

Uncle Adam looked straight at Chloe. "Then I'll finally die."

Chloe was in shock.

"Why, Uncle Adam? Why do you want to die?"

"I am tired, Chloe." He had tears in his eyes. "I can't breathe. They pump oxygen into me. My heart is barely working. I am always in pain, and when the painkillers kick in I can't do anything. Hell, I can't even think straight. I am not functioning properly. I can't go on like this any longer."

Q. Should Chloe help Uncle Adam die?

No. It's not her decision. It's not her body.

Yes. It's his body, it's his decision and he decided to do that. He just asked her to help him.

"Uncle Adam, I can't do that," Chloe was also crying.

"Why not?"

"I just can't."

She turned her wheelchair. "I have to go."

"Stay, Chloe."

She turned the wheelchair back. They were quiet for a moment. Uncle Adam was resting. Then he rose on his pillow. "Chloe, why did you ask me your question?"

"Somebody asked me. I have to give the answer tonight and I have no idea what the right answer is."

"Is it important for you?"

"Yes, very important."

"Stay a little longer. I'll try to help you with your question."

"Thank you."

"It's up to you to come up with an answer that satisfies you, but I can help you to think about it."

"Great, Uncle Adam."

Uncle Adam asked her to pass him a pen and paper and started making notes while talking to her.

"What exactly was the question?"

"What my most important job is."

She noticed that he wrote "most important job."

"But you are not working yet, are you?"

"No, but there were alternative formulations."

"What were those?"

"What my main responsibility in life is. What the most important thing I should be concerned about is. If I am allowed to focus on only one thing, what it is."

"Ok." He repeated several times as if tasting each word. "Your. Most important. Job. Your. Most important. Job." He wrote down "Your" and underlined it. Then he said, "Think of something that you can do better than anybody else. Or better yet that only you can do it." He asked, "Do you agree?"

"Yes," answered Chloe.

Next, he wrote and underlined "Most important." He thought a little and said,

146

"Think of an activity without which any other activity cannot be done well. Or better yet cannot be done at all."

"I'll try," said Chloe.

Finally, he wrote down and underlined "Job." He looked at the math books around him and said, "Think of something that you should be doing all the time and all your life."

Q. Can you think of the answer that satisfies the conditions that Uncle Adam formulated?

Kevin's attorney

While Chloe rolled back to her room in her wheelchair, suddenly a young blond woman with large black shades covering her face and with a large black briefcase in her arm stood in front of Chloe. "I am Diana Barrera, representing Kevin. I have an offer for you: admit that you were driving the car during the accident or your mother goes to jail."

"You want me to lie and go to jail or else you threaten to jail my mother?" asked Chloe.

"Yes, but, as a minor, you will be immediately pardoned by the governor," said the woman. "You know that he is Kevin's father?"

Q. Should Chloe accept the offer?

Yes. Nothing will happen to her, but otherwise her mother will be in jail. It's all her fault anyway.

No. That would be a lie. And a lie to law enforcement officials is most probably a crime. Even if Kevin's attorney is telling the truth and will keep her promise—which is uncertain—it's impossible to predict all the consequences that will result from this lie. Chloe and her family are already in deep trouble because of little lies that she made.

"Go away," said Chloe quietly, almost whispering.

"What?"

"Go away," she almost screamed.

"What's going on?" Arif jumped between them. Behind him Chloe's doctor was talking on the phone.

The woman turned and left.

"Where did you go?" asked Arif. For the first time since Chloe met him he wasn't smiling.

Chloe was surprised to see him angry. Hadn't he helped her to make that little trip?

"I was around," said Chloe defiantly.

"Who let you go?"

Chloe wanted to say "you," but decided to discharge the situation with a joke. "Do you see a pacifier in my mouth?"

"Wh-a-a-t?"

"I am not a baby. I don't have to ask for permission." She was astonished to see such a change in his attitude, and she didn't understand why he was pretending to not be aware of where she had been. Or was their previous conversation just a meaningless exercise of pleasantries on his part and he really wasn't aware? Or was he just covering his behind because the doctor was there? Anyway, her joke didn't help. Arif was furious.

"Do you know that you have an operation tomorrow?"

"What operation?"

"Your leg amputation," he pointed to her knee.

"Why?" Chloe burst into tears. "Why?"

"You didn't know? I just found about it, but I thought you knew all along." Arif was taken aback.

"You are lying," whispered Chloe. Her throat tightened, she was fighting tears. "Tell me the truth!"

"I... don't... know, maybe the doctor will save it." He clearly regretted that he had blurted it out. At this moment, the doctor put down his phone and asked Chloe, "What's going on?" Chloe didn't answer.

He turned to Arif. "Did you upset her?"

"No!"

The doctor looked at Chloe and asked, "Why are you crying?"

Q. Should Chloe tell the truth?

Yes. Of course. Why should she cover up for Arif? He didn't talk about the operation to help Chloe; he did it to blame her. Why should she lie to the doctor now?

No. People were hiding important information from Chloe. It means they lied to her. So she can lie back. All she would be doing is not disclosing that somebody made her aware of their lies.

Chloe rolled her wheelchair forward and they both stepped aside. Arif followed her into her room. Chloe took the headscarf off and gave it back to him.

Q. Did she make the right decision giving back the headscarf?

Yes. Arif had betrayed her. He lied in front of the doctor pretending that he didn't know where she went, hiding that he helped her to go visit Uncle Adam. It's understandable that she doesn't want to wear gifts from a traitor and a liar.

No. It was important for her to stay in this hospital. It was so important that she even decided to lie about being a Muslim. She was probably afraid that she would suffer physical harm if she hadn't lied and didn't wear that headscarf. If it was so important, why does she take it off now? Even if Arif is a bad man, it doesn't mean that the headscarf is bad, does it? And once he gave it to her, it became hers; the headscarf had nothing to do with Arif anymore.

Without saying another word, Arif helped her to get to her bed, and connected her IV tubing. Then he said, "I am sorry." Chloe didn't answer and he left.

It was late at night. It was raining outside and Chloe was quietly crying and looking as the drops attacked the window with their entire bodies and then splattered and fell. And immediately other drops took their place. She remembered that in French class they studied a poem *Il Pleure dans mon Coeur*, which meant it rains in my heart. It also meant it cries in my heart.

She was looking at the rain hitting the windows when all-of-a-sudden she realized that she knew the answer to both questions. For the first time that day she was calm. She closed her eyes, turned away from the window, and immediately fell asleep.

The series continues...

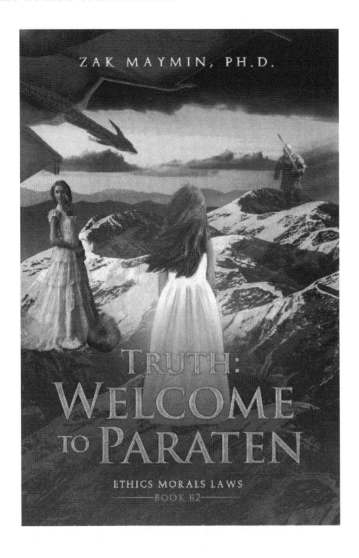

Made in the USA
Columbia, SC
30 November 2020